owep

As You Grow

The story of Sky Tree

BRAVE
BOOKS

DOM-A-TRON

THE OLD ISLAN...

Doomsdome

Burrycanter

UTOPIA

Freedom Island

WIGGAMORE

SUMA SAVANNA

Rushington

Furenzy Park

Hi...

Toke-A-Toke

Wonder Well

Co...

Mushroom Village

Deserted Desert

Mt. Avalerif

Sky Tree

RAKA RAIN FOREST

Snapfast Meadow

CAR-A-LAGO COAST

Starlotte City

Gray Landing

Home of the Brave

Welcome to Freedom Island, Home of the Brave, where good battles evil and truth prevails. Learn about love, joy, and gentleness and then complete the BRAVE Challenge at the end of the book.

Watch this video for an introduction to the story and BRAVE Universe!

Saga Two: Iron Chaos
Book 8

As You Grow

Map Labels:
- Shivermore
- Nogard Cavern
- MONOCK MOUNTAINS
- Meltonville
- Way
- CABAL ISLAND
- Temple of the Serpent

Saga Two: Iron Chaos—Book 8

As You Grow

Book Illustrations © 2022 by Juan Moreno
Map Illustration © 2021 by Ali Elzeiny

Published by BRAVE BOOKS
www.BRAVEbooks.com

ISBN: 978-1-955550-29-1 (paperback)

First edition published in the USA in 2022 by BRAVE BOOKS

Printed in Canada

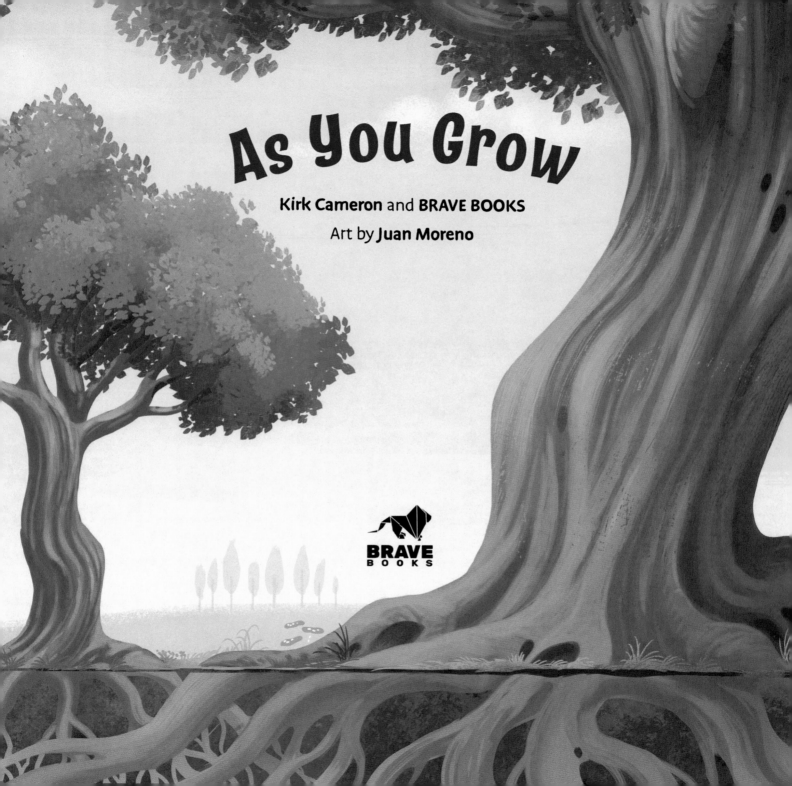

As You Grow

Kirk Cameron and BRAVE BOOKS

Art by Juan Moreno

BRAVE BOOKS

As seasons change, you will grow.
Spread your branches and put down
roots like in this story of Sky Tree.
As you do, let your fruit be sweet.

You are very small but very loved.

You were made to
point up to the One
who loves you best.

Sometimes love hurts,
but love is always
worth it.

Because you've been cared for, care for others.

A tender word is soft, and it gives life like a spring rain.

When you've grown big, be excited to join something bigger than yourself.

But always take time to enjoy the little things.

As you grow,
you will know sorrow ...

But brokenness is never the end.

Remember that the greatest sorrow
can lead to the greatest joy.

As you grow strong,
grow in gentleness.

Let your strength and gentleness be what draws others to you.

In all these things,
find comfort as you grow.

BRAVE Cadets,

Sky Tree and the animals that live there have been through many seasons of life. As you grow, you will go through many seasons as well. Complete the BRAVE Challenge to learn more about the love, joy, and gentleness that will help you on your journey!

- Help Sky Tree and the animals in the BRAVE games, and celebrate your victory with an epic reward.

  - See if you can find at least 10 owls in the story!

Are you ready to grow and be BRAVE?

THE BRAVE CHALLENGE

INTRODUCING...
KIRK CAMERON

Kirk Cameron, a Christian, producer, actor, loving husband, and father, is an icon in the television and film industry. Additionally, Kirk has had a big impact in our society through films like *Fireproof*, *Lifemark*, and *Homeschool Awakening*. He and his wife, Chelsea, live in California and have six children. Kirk Cameron has joined with BRAVE Books in creating this special book on growth and the Fruit of the Spirit, *As You Grow*.

KIRK SUGGESTS:

"I hope you and your family will be blessed with this story as it teaches about growth and the importance of love, joy, and gentleness."

INTRODUCTION

Sky Tree is in danger! Your mission for this BRAVE Challenge is to save Sky Tree from the evil tiger, Black Heart. To get started, grab a sheet of paper and a pencil, and draw a scoreboard like the one shown.

In the end, if your team can put more points on this scoreboard than Black Heart, you have won the challenge and saved Sky Tree.

Before starting Game #1, choose a prize for winning. For example ...

- Buying a plant to take care of as a family
- Visiting the zoo or a park
- Making an apple pie
- Whatever gets your kiddos excited!

BRAVE Cadets	Black Heart
⩝⩝⩝ II	III

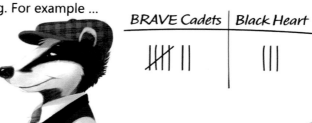

> "But the fruit of the Spirit is love, joy, peace, patience, kindness, goodness, faithfulness, gentleness, self-control; against such things there is no law."
>
> **Galatians 5:22-23** (ESV)

Fruit of the Spirit: LOVE

GAME #1 - LOVE-N-LEARN

LESSON

Love looks for ways to serve others, even if that means sacrificing its own desires.

OBJECTIVE

Sky Tree displayed love to all of the animals by giving of itself sacrificially. BRAVE Cadets, in this game, you'll need to give up your desires in order to serve those around you, too.

MATERIALS

A ball and all of the cadets favorite pillows, blankets, and stuffed animals.

INSTRUCTIONS

ROUND 1:

1. Have the cadets fill their arms with blankets, pillows, and stuffed animals until they can't hold anything else.

2. *Secret Step: Parents, add more of their stuff into their hands, on their head, and between their arms. Make sure that they actually can't hold anything else.*

3. The cadets must walk around the room without letting anything fall. They may not stop moving.

4. A parent will toss a ball to the moving cadet. The cadet must try to catch it without dropping any of the objects.

5. ***Secret Step:*** *It should be impossible for the cadets to catch more than what they already have.*

ROUND 2:

6. Now, tell the cadets to drop half of their objects.

7. Throw the ball to each cadet again. They should be able to catch the ball now.

SCORING

If at least one BRAVE Cadet successfully catches the ball during the game, the cadets receive 5 points.

Black Heart receives 1 point for each item dropped when attempting to catch the ball.

Award the BRAVE Cadets with a total of 5 points if at least one cadet successfully catches the ball.

TALK ABOUT IT

1. What do you think it means to love one another?

KIRK SUGGESTS:

"Loving others involves sacrificing your own time, desires, or plans to serve someone else. Love isn't just a feeling; it's a way to actively put others before yourself. Ephesians 2:1–4 says, 'Therefore if you have … any comfort from his love … then make my joy complete by being like-minded, having the same love …. Do nothing out of selfish ambition or vain conceit. Rather, in humility value others above yourselves, not looking to your own interests but each of you to the interests of the others.'"

2. In the game, you had to be able to catch a ball while your arms were filled with your favorite blankets, pillows, and stuffed animals. Were you able to easily catch the ball while carrying those objects? What happened when you gave up some of your objects?

3. Is it easy to give up your possessions or desires to serve someone else? What would make it easier or harder?

4. In the story, Sky Tree gave one of its branches as a crutch for an injured capybara. How is that showing love to the capybara? Did the tree expect anything in return for helping the capybara?

5. How did the capybara show his appreciation for the tree's help? What are some ways that you can show your appreciation for the people who love you?

KIRK SUGGESTS:

"Sometimes it's hard to love someone who doesn't show love to you. Instead of responding with unkindness, look for ways to serve them."

6. The strongest kind of love is unconditional love. What would this kind of love look like? Give an example of unconditional love.

KIRK SUGGESTS:

"Sometimes it's hard to love unconditionally when a sibling acts selfishly or acts out of anger towards you. Respond with love and service instead of being angry back at them. Jesus is the perfect example of unconditional love because of what He did for us on the cross. Romans 5:8 says, 'But God shows his love for us in that while we were still sinners, Christ died for us.'"

GAME #2 - A JOYFUL MATCH

LESSON

A joyful person chooses to respond to adversity with the right perspective and seeks to give joy to others.

MATERIALS

A few pieces of paper, a pen, and scissors.

OBJECTIVE

Sky Tree has just been attacked by Black Heart and the animals' homes have been destroyed! BRAVE Cadets, help the animals choose to respond rightly to the hardship by identifying the good or bad responses.

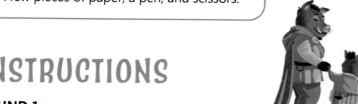

INSTRUCTIONS

ROUND 1:

1. Cut up the paper into 20 equal-sized squares, and write each of the words twice from the list of 10 words on the next page.

2. Shuffle the pieces of paper and lay them face down on the table in rows.

3. The cadets take turns flipping over 2 pieces of paper at a time. If the words match, they take the 2 words and go again.

4. If they flip over 2 pieces of paper and the words don't match, then replace the papers face down and let the next cadet have a turn.

BRAVE TIP

The trick is to remember where all the words are in order to match them correctly.

ROUND 2:

5. Mix up the cards and repeat the matching process but have the cadets try to match the words that they think are the opposites of each other.

6. There will be two of each opposite pair on the table.

SECRET BRAVE TIP

Key for the opposite pairs: Joy/sadness, gratitude/discontentment, peace/anxiety, kind-heartedness/anger, bitterness/forgiveness.

LIST

1. Joy
2. Gratitude
3. Peace
4. Kind-heartedness
5. Bitterness

6. Sadness
7. Discontentment
8. Anxiety
9. Anger
10. Forgiveness

SCORING

If the cadets flip the correct match, they receive a point.
If the cadets flip the wrong match, Black Heart receives a point.

TALK ABOUT IT

1. What do you think it means to be joyful? In what situations should we be joyful? (For example, only when things are going well?)

KIRK SUGGESTS:

"Being joyful doesn't always mean being happy. It can mean that there is hope even when things are hard. It's choosing to be joyful in those hard times that is pleasing to God. James 1:2-3 says, 'Count it all joy, my brothers, when you meet trials of various kinds, for you know that the testing of your faith produces steadfastness.'"

2. In the game, you had to correctly choose the opposite responses that go together. In hardships, we can choose how we respond. (Some responses are mentioned in the game.) How do you respond in a time of hardship?

3. In the story, the animals living in Sky Tree had their homes destroyed by Black Heart. What did they do in response to the hard situation? What did they choose to do instead of getting revenge?

4. Can you think of a time when you felt really sad but chose to be joyful? Did choosing to be joyful help the situation or the feelings of those around you?

5. What are some life-giving words or actions that you can offer to bring someone else joy or gladness (to your family, teammates, classmates, church, city, nation)?

KIRK SUGGESTS:

"When you show joy and thankfulness in every situation, you can be an encouragement to others as well."

GAME #3 - BE GENTLE OR BE WET

LESSON

Gentleness is using your strength in a way that humbly seeks to show kindness in word and action.

OBJECTIVE

The animals living in Sky Tree are rebuilding their city after the attack from Black Heart. BRAVE Cadets, help the animals learn that gentleness is necessary in order to protect the relationships with **those** around them.

MATERIALS

Balloons, water, and a bucket or large bowl. If you don't have water balloons, play this game with eggs.

INSTRUCTIONS

1. The BRAVE Cadets must carefully toss water balloons to each other.

2. Fill a few balloons with water, and place them in a bucket.

BRAVE TIP

This game should be played outside.

3. Have the cadets break up into pairs and stand an arm's length away from each other.

BRAVE TIP

If there is an odd number of cadets, pair one with a parent.

4. Complete 5 rounds of tossing their balloon to a partner and back. After each round, have each partner take 2 big steps back from one another and then toss the balloon again.

5. Every time a balloon or breaks, the cadets lose points. If the balloon breaks before finishing 5 rounds, the cadets can get another water balloon and continue from the round you are on.

BRAVE TIP

The goal is for the cadets to learn that sometimes being gentle is better than using force.

ONE CHILD MODIFICATION

Have the cadet and the parent toss the water balloon to each other. The rules are the same.

SCORING

If a water balloon drops on the floor but doesn't break, Black Heart receives 1 point. If a water balloon drops and breaks, Black Heart receives 2 points.
For every toss that the cadets don't drop or break the balloons, they receive 2 points.

TALK ABOUT IT

1. What do you think gentleness means?

KIRK SUGGESTS:

"Gentleness is being kind, humble, and caring rather than being mean or harsh to those around you in both your words and actions. Proverbs 15:4 ESV says, 'A gentle tongue is a tree of life, but perverseness in it breaks the spirit.'"

2. In the game, you had to carefully toss a water balloon to your partner. Why did you have to toss the balloon gently? If the water balloon in the game represents our relationships with the people in our lives, how can we be gentle and protect those around us? Is repairing a broken relationship like trying to fix a broken water balloon?

3. How do most people respond when someone is angry at them? How do you usually respond? Why is it important to respond with gentleness?

KIRK SUGGESTS:

"Most people respond with defensiveness or holding a grudge. It's important to not respond to anger with anger. Proverbs 15:1 ESV says, 'A soft answer turns away wrath, but a harsh word stirs up anger.'"

4. Do people usually see gentleness as a weakness or a strength? Why? How is it a strength?

5. No matter how small or young you are, you can still show gentleness. What are some ways that you can show gentleness to those who are younger than you?

6. Who is someone that you know that shows gentleness? What do they do that shows gentleness? What are some ways that you can follow their example?

KIRK SUGGESTS:

"Jesus is the ultimate example of gentleness. He cared for the young, weak, sick, and the outcasts. Matthew 11:28–29 says, 'Come to me, all who labor and are heavy laden, and I will give you rest. Take my yoke upon you, and learn from me, for I am gentle and lowly in heart, and you will find rest for your souls.'"

TALLY UP THE POINTS TO SEE IF YOU WON!

FINAL THOUGHTS FROM KIRK CAMERON

The Fruit of the Spirit are characteristics that we all should seek in order to be like Jesus Christ. Love is a way to serve someone else and sacrifice your time and desires for them without expecting anything in return. Being joyful in everything you do means to have hope in the hard times and to trust that God has everything in control. Gentleness is being kind and humble to those around you in both words and actions, no matter what. As we seek to be loving, joyful, and gentle, we must examine our words, thoughts, and actions towards those around us. Parents, you have the opportunity to model these qualities of Jesus Christ as an example for your children.

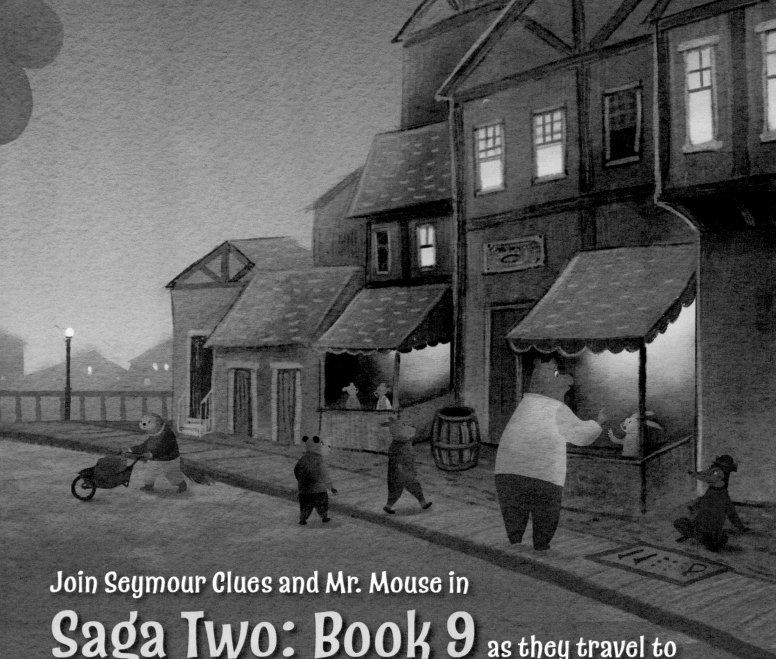

Join Seymour Clues and Mr. Mouse in
Saga Two: Book 9 as they travel to
Gray Landing, uncovering one mystery after another.

Made in the USA
Coppell, TX
31 May 2023

17505894R00031